Hunter's Tail Vol. 1

A Dog's Guide to Teaching Children Lessons of Love
"Listen to your Heart. It Always Knows Best."

Hunter's Tail: A Dog's Guide to Teaching Children Lessons of Love
by: Andy Pavarini

Copyright © 2016 by Andy Pavarini

Published by
Christine F. Anderson Publishing & Media, Madison VA, 22727
www.publishwithcfa.com

CHRISTINE F. ANDERSON

ISBN: 978-0692958018

Printed in the United States of America

Hunter's Tail

A Dog's Guide to Teaching Children Lessons of Love
"Listen to Your Heart, It Always Knows Best"

By Hunter's Paw,
Andy Pavarini

Hunter's Tail

Dedication

This book is dedicated to my super spectacular friend and love, Kathleen Rubi. As children we dream of a time in the future when we will meet our human soul mate, and Kathleen is mine. I consider a soul mate someone who you feel understands your heart; the authentic person of kindness and goodness that each of us truly are as expressed through a loving symbol.

Kathleen sees the real me when others can't, understands who I am even when I don't, and supports me unconditionally with love from her heart no matter what. Kathleen is my best friend forever (BFF) and I am so grateful that she has chosen to share her amazing self, and her life filled with hope and compassion for everyone, with little ol' me!

Kathleen and Mr. Tucker, Hunter's brother and best friend

chapter 1

Hello, I'm Hunter!

Hello there, and welcome to the magical adventures of *Hunter's Tail*, by me, Mr. Hunter! Before we get too far, there's something you should know about me: I'm a dog.

And because I'm a dog, I tell my tails a little differently. See, I already started! When a dog tells a tale, we call it a tail. And this book you have in your hands is full of my tails, all about my life. I learned a lot, and I want to share it all with you!

Have you ever heard someone say, "You can't teach an old dog new tricks?" Well, that might be true, but this old dog is going to teach you a new trick or two. But first, there are a couple other things I need to tell you.

This book is all about love. Dogs are practically made of love. Did you know that? If you have a dog, then you might know what I mean. Dogs just love to love!

Don't believe me? I want you to try something. Next time you're sad or angry, go give your dog a big hug. I bet you can't stay sad or angry for very long!

You see, dogs are here for two reasons. The first one is to love you. The second reason is to teach you how to love. You might not know what I mean just yet, but after you read my tails, I think you'll get the idea.

Now let me tell you a couple of things about me. I'm a yellow Labrador, so I'm a pretty big dog, with lots of golden-colored fur. I'm a little bit chunky, because I LOVE peanut-butter treats . . . they're my favorite thing in the world! I love them so much that I want to share them with everyone, so when I say, "Peanut-butter treat for you!" that's the same as saying, "Good job! You deserve an award!"

My Paw tells me that human children like gold-star stickers and candy, but believe me, there's nothing better than a delicious peanut-butter treat!

Oh, right, I should tell you. My human's name is Andy, but I call him Paw. That's my name for him, just like he calls me Hunter, or Mr. Hunter, or sometimes Pup Pup, or Misters . . . I have a lot of different names!

I sniffed this whole book to my Paw Andy, and he wrote it all down for me. See, dogs don't "say" things like people do. Instead, we "sniff" things. I bet you've seen two dogs meet each other, right? What do they do? They sniff each other. That's their way of saying, "Hello! It's so nice to meet you!"

Each of these tails you're about to read is a story about me and my Paw Andy, and each tail has a lesson in it. And each lesson has something to do with . . . guess what? That's right—love! You're going to see that word a lot in this book. It doesn't always mean that you love something the way you love your parents, or the way I love peanut-butter treats. Sometimes love can be as simple as thinking good thoughts. Sometimes love means that you forgive someone for doing something, even if it made you feel bad. And other times, love is doing something nice for someone, even if you don't get anything in return.

There are so many different kinds of love, and we're going to explore them all. Are you ready to hear my tails? Then let's go!

chapter 2

Dogs and People... Who Really Chooses Who?

You might think that people pick their dogs. I'm sorry to tell you, but this is just not true.

Maybe you go to a pet store, or an animal shelter, or a dog breeder, and you think you choose the right dog for you ... but really, that dog already knows that you're going to pick him or her. They're just waiting for you to come along and get them!

Let me tell you about how my Paw Andy found me—or actually, how I found him.

I was born on December 12, on a farm during a cold winter. The people who owned the farm were named Iven and Sue. Iven was a very kind man who took good care of my doggie parents. My dad's name was Sir Lancelot Buckwheat. (Go ahead, try to say that out loud without giggling!) My mom's name was Homestead Amanda.

Both of my parents were beautiful Labradors with yellow-colored fur. Before me and my brothers and sisters came along, my parents spent summers in big, green fields, and their winters inside a big, warm building. They would get oatmeal bubble baths and loved to spend time with their humans, Iven and Sue. They had a good life!

Both of my parents were yellow, but when my mom had puppies, we all came out in different colors. Some of us were all white. Some were all black. Some were chocolate, which means they were a rich brown color that made people think of yummy chocolate. (Mr. Hunter isn't allowed to eat chocolate, because it makes dogs sick, but it sure smells good!) As for me, I was born with my fur all yellow, just like my parents.

In our doggie family, I wasn't the biggest, or the strongest, or the cutest, but that didn't matter. All dogs love each other, even if we look different. We always help each other. That's the very first lesson you can learn from a dog. It doesn't matter if someone looks different than you, or if they're smaller or bigger or just not the same as you—you should never judge someone just for that.

How would you feel if someone didn't like you because you were different from them? I bet it wouldn't feel very good. If you can learn one thing from a dog, it's that you should "love without condition." That means you love no matter if someone else is a different size or a different color, or if they're a boy or a girl. And when you do that, when you love without condition, you will see that love comes back to you!

Iven's barn on the farm was warm and cozy, and he took such good care of our family. There were six of us puppies, and by the time we were eight weeks old we learned how to walk. We would sniff and play and sometimes get into things we weren't supposed to.

But soon, three of my brothers and sisters left to go be with their human families. I was sad to see them go, but I knew that the whole reason they came here in the first place was to be with humans, and love them, and teach them how to love. So even though I was sad to see them go, I was also happy that they found their humans.

Then it was my time. I knew I was ready, and I was going to do everything I could to make my human know how lucky I was to pick him. See, when I say "I picked him," I mean that I already knew that this human, Andy, had some problems in his life, and he really needed to learn how to love!

But then, outside, a snow storm started. I began to worry. What if my human couldn't make it in this terrible storm? What if he changed his mind and decided he didn't want a dog after all? No, I sniffed to myself. I picked him, after all. He had to come.

Then the door to the barn opened and a chilly wind blew in. And I heard Iven say, "Hi Andy! Come right in and meet your new pup!"

chapter 3
Puppy Love

Dogs always think good thoughts. That's why our tails are almost always wagging! But even when our tails are not wagging, we're still full of happiness and love. It's simple: good thoughts bring good things. Because dogs always think good thoughts, we're always happy, and it's even easier to love.

When you think bad thoughts, or angry thoughts, you bring on bad things. That might sound silly, but really, think about it for a minute! When your thoughts are sad or angry, all your NEW thoughts are sad or angry too, and nothing feels good. If you look at everything positively, nothing can get you down!

This was a lesson my new Paw Andy needed to learn.

When Andy walked into the barn that day in winter when I was just a pup, I looked at his face and I knew he was my human. I tried to run over to him, but my paws were very big and I was very small, so I tripped.

Then Andy picked me up and he looked at me, and he said, "That's my dog."

And I sniffed, "That's my human!"

It was still snowing outside, so my new human Paw was extra careful on the drive home. My new home!

Everything was wonderful in my new home, and Paw Andy took good care of me. But very soon I could see why my human needed me to love him and teach him how to love. See, Paw Andy had a very hard job, and sometimes little things made him frustrated or angry. He didn't understand yet why it was so important to love and be loved.

Humans are not here on earth to be sad and tired and frustrated. Humans are supposed to be happy, just like dogs! Just remember that nobody is perfect. I'm not perfect, and you aren't either. We shouldn't try to be perfect. We should just try to be happy and loving!

Sometimes I would come into a room and see that my Paw Andy was having bad thoughts because his usual smile looked like a frown. So I would go over to him with my big puppy paws and nudge him and sniff, "I love you! Love me back right now or I will stare at you until you hug me!" And soon he would hug me, and then he would smile because he knew that I loved him.

It didn't take Paw Andy very long to know that I was sent to him so that he could find peace and love, and be loved. If you have a dog, go give him or her a hug and a kiss on the snout, and tell them you love them too! Yes, tell them. Dogs can feel your energy shine, and when a human says, "I love you," those words feel amazing to a dog. And of course to humans too!

Do you remember in Chapter 1 when I said that Mr. Hunter would teach you a new trick or two? Here's one right now. This is something that anybody can do when they're feeling angry or sad or frustrated. And it's so easy! All it takes is thirty seconds, and you can do it anytime. Here's how it works.

First, close your eyes and take some deep breaths.

Next, think about the happiest you have ever been. Maybe it was your birthday, or a trip with your family, or maybe just a good time with your best friend.

Then, really THINK about that happy time. Make it play like a movie in your mind. Who was there? Where were you? How did you feel? You can feel that way again, right now.

Okay ready? For each person that was there, think about their face. Were they smiling? Were they laughing? What did they look like, having this great time with you? How did that make you feel?

Think about all the love you felt at that one time. There were no problems, right? No feelings of sadness or anger? Stay in that moment, in that movie in your mind of that great time. Nothing else matters right now.

The last step is to open your eyes and take another really deep breath. Then let it out.

🐾 Andy Pavarini 🐾

Do you feel better? I bet you do! Good job . . . Peanut-butter treat for you!

That's just one thing you can do anytime you feel sad or angry, and Mr. Hunter promises it will make you feel better. I know it sure helped my Paw Andy!

chapter 4
Healing for People and Dogs

Maybe you've heard someone say, "Give and you shall receive." Some people might think that this means if you give something, you get something. But that's not it at all! It means that if you do things for other people and give love, you'll get love back.

Life with my Paw Andy was great. By the time I was two years old, Andy was learning all about how to love, and I was learning all about the world.

Then one day, my Paw told me, "Hunter, we are going to volunteer our time!"

At first, I didn't know what that word "volunteer" meant. To volunteer means that you spend some time doing something, but you don't want money or anything for it. When you volunteer, you do something because you want to help. And I bet you guessed this already, but volunteering and helping others is just another way to show love.

Andy got me a nice, new blue collar (blue is Mr. Hunter's favorite color) and a fancy harness. He gave me an oatmeal-shampoo bath so I smelled good, and then he took me to a big building I had never seen before.

Inside were lots of other dogs in all shapes and sizes. I met another dog named Chewy and we became friends right away. All of us dogs had to learn new tricks, like how to sit, and stay, and lay down, and bark or not bark. We had to learn not to sniff humans when they walked by. The hardest trick to learn was to stay calm when there was a loud or scary noise. I messed up at first, but I'm a fast learner! They say "Practice makes perfect!"

I didn't know yet why we needed to learn all these things. Before I could find out, there was a test. Can you believe that? Even dogs have to take tests! I had to follow Paw Andy and listen to what he said. I had to stop when he stopped, and I had to sit when he said "Sit."

Of course, I passed my test! Mr. Hunter is smarter than your average pup.

Andy gave me a thumbs-up for passing my test, and my new friend Chewy gave me a high-paw ... which is like a high-five for dogs, because we don't have fingers. My Paw was so proud! He petted me and gave me kisses, and then he told me, "Congratulations, Hunter! You are now a therapy dog for sick children."

Therapy dog? I didn't know what that was. I sure was learning a lot. See, "therapy" is something that helps to heal someone or make them feel better. So a therapy dog is a dog that visits with sick people and helps them feel better by making them happy. And Pup Pup was going to be a therapy dog for children!

See, even though Andy was my human and I was his dog, that didn't mean that I couldn't love other humans too. We were going to volunteer and give our time to children in need. And Mr. Hunter just loves children! I was so excited my tail was swish-swishing back and forth. I couldn't wait to get started!

chapter 5

Would You Trade Your Troubles with Someone Else?

I sniffed it before, and I'll sniff it again: Nobody is perfect. That is so important to know. Everybody has problems, and we like to think that our problems are more important than other people's problems. But that's simply not true! Everybody's problems are important, because they are THEIR problems.

So what can you do when someone you know has a problem? There is only one thing to do: Love without condition. Love no matter what, and that love will come back to you. It's a lot like volunteering; when you give something, you get something, even if you don't expect to get something.

Now that I was a therapy dog, once every week my Paw Andy would give me my favorite oatmeal-shampoo bath, and then we would get in the car and go to meet the children. Other therapy dogs were there, like my friend Chewy, and we would sniff and wag our tails every time we saw each other.

Then we would get on an elevator. Mr. Hunter didn't like the elevator at first, but after a couple of times, I got used to it. Finally, we would go into a big playroom with chairs, couches, toys, and lots of space.

After all the therapy dogs were in the big playroom, the doctors would bring in the children. There were so many of them, and they were all so different—boys and girls of all ages and sizes and colors. But they all had one thing in common. They all had a smile so big I could hardly see anything else. These children were so beautiful in my eyes and we were the luckiest dogs because we chose to help them feel a little bit better. Close your eyes and imagine how happy you would feel to see us dogs if we were visiting you.

I said before in the last chapter that all of these children were sick, and that made Mr. Hunter very sad. But these children were all so happy to play with us therapy dogs that it was like nothing was wrong at all. There was so much joy and love in that big playroom that my tail never stopped wagging!

At first I wanted to just run over and start playing with the kids right away, but because I had training as a therapy dog, I knew I had to wait for the children to come to me. So I sat like a good boy and waited. And sure enough, the kids came over with their big smiles and they chose which dog they wanted to play with.

Of course Mr. Hunter got picked every time!

Soon the room was filled with laughing and playing. It was the most beautiful time I had ever seen. These children loved the therapy dogs, and us dogs loved them back.

Now there was nothing that I could do about these children being sick. Mr. Hunter is not a doctor (or else they would call me Dr. Hunter!) but for that time every week I could love them, and they could love me. I was giving and receiving at the same time. And that's what love is all about!

chapter 6

Be Part of Something Bigger

Mr. Hunter wants to share with you a very special tail about my time as a therapy dog. You see, sometimes we need to "be part of something bigger" than ourselves. What does that mean?

That means that even though you have your own life, and you probably have your own troubles, sometimes we need to put them aside because we are a small part of a bigger thing that might be more important than we think.

I know, that's a tough idea, right? I hope that this tail will help you understand what I mean.

One night, while I was a therapy dog, me and my Paw Andy were waiting for the children to come into the big playroom. Very soon, the room was filled with laughter and smiles, like it always was. But there was one little girl that was looking right at me.

This little girl's name was Michelle, and she was the most adorable girl I ever saw. Michelle was in a wheelchair, but that did not slow her down. She rolled along at such a speed she almost knocked me over!

Michelle had big green eyes and a wide, wonderful smile. She put her small arms around my neck and gave me one of the best hugs ever.

She said, "Hi, I'm Michelle! What's your name?"

My Paw Andy told her, "Hi, Michelle. It's nice to meet you. This is Mr. Hunter."

"Oh, I just love you, Mr. Hunter!" Michelle said. "I just love you!"

Me and Michelle played and played. She giggled when I licked her face, and my tail never stopped wagging. But soon I had to go home. Michelle wanted to keep me there forever! But my Paw told her that we would come back in a week to play some more.

Every week we came back, and every week Michelle picked me as her therapy dog. She would always give me a great big hug, squeezing me for at least twenty seconds. Then she would say, "Oh, I just love you, Mr. Hunter! I just love you!"

For months and months me and my Paw would visit with Michelle. Then one day we came and Michelle was not there anymore. That made us both very sad, but I know that Michelle is in a better place. And I also know she has plenty of other pups to play with!

Now I can tell you what I meant about being part of something bigger. Mr. Hunter was just a small part of Michelle's life. But for an hour each week, I know she felt loved. You can be a part of something bigger too. It's easy—all you have to do is help someone feel loved!

Mr. Hunters wants to let you know that choices you make in life can really make other people feel loved. If you choose to give and receive love, your life will be filled with happiness no matter what happens. Love is always the answer to a happy heart. You can do it!

chapter 7

A Dog Only Needs His Human

As a dog, Mr. Hunter doesn't need much. All I really need is my human, and some yummy peanut-butter treats. (Okay, I guess I don't NEED them.) Of course I want naps and playtime and walks in the park . . . but I don't need them. So when I do get those things, they are a gift, and I like to be thankful for them.

Humans don't need much either. But a lot of times, you spend too much time thinking about what you want, and you don't stop to think about what you have. Everything in life is a gift, from love to food to friends to family. For everything that you have, there's someone else out there that doesn't have it. And yes, being happy with the things you have is another type of love!

When Mr. Hunter was around two years old, my Paw Andy decided that we were going to move to Arizona, which is a state waaay on the other side of the country from Maryland where I was born. So we packed up the car, and we took a trip to live out west!

It was a great road trip. We saw lots of amazing things, and we ate good food, and my Paw told me stories the whole time.

When we arrived in Arizona, boy was it hot! But it was okay, because there was so much to see and do. There were spiny cactus plants, and beautiful red and brown mountains, and new parks to explore.

I was happy, but I could tell that Andy was not sure. See, he thought that moving me to a new place might not be good for me. And my Paw does not speak dog, so I couldn't just sniff, "Hey, I like it here!"

What could I do? I'll tell you: I showed him that it didn't matter where we lived, or what we had. The only thing I needed was my human. Wherever he was, I would be happy! Everything else is just "icing on the cake."

Take some time to think about what you need in your life. It might be that some things you think you NEED are actually just things you WANT. Next, take a minute to think about all the things you have, whether you needed them or just wanted them. Last, Mr. Hunter wants you to think about how happy it makes you feel to know that you have all that you enough to be happy. I hope that you feel thankful for all of those gifts. If you do, great job—peanut-butter treat for you!

Here's one more trick that Misters wants to share with you. When you're feeling frustrated or negative, say this sentence: "*One, two, three, let my thoughts and feelings flee!*"

Then smile, or laugh, and think about how you have everything you need. And be happy!

chapter 8
Hunter Gets a Brother

If you're lucky, you might have brothers or sisters. Mr. Hunter knows that sometimes brothers and sisters don't get along very well, especially in humans, but they can be the best thing that ever happened to you! If you don't have any brothers or sisters, then you probably have cousins, or a best friend, or maybe even two best friends. What Mr. Hunter is trying to say is that nobody has to be alone. Everyone should share their love with others! And yes, you can love a friend just like you love a brother or sister.

One day, when Paw Andy and I were living in Arizona, he came home with a very special surprise. He was carrying a little furball in his arms—another dog! Mr. Hunter got a little brother that day. He was just a little pup, and his name was Tucker. I was so excited that I almost knocked poor Tucker over the first time I ran towards him to play.

Tucker was a Labrador, just like me, just a little darker yellow closer to a golden-brown. But Tucker was afraid of a lot of things. He got scared when there was thunder and lightning, and he would run and hide under the bed. Loud noises scared him too, even when it was sunny and warm out.

I found out later that Tucker used to be a homeless dog—that means he did not have a human or a home. When he was young, he was all by himself out in the wild. He did not get to eat much, and there was nobody to give him yummy peanut-butter treats! He did not feel loved by anyone, so he was sad. One time, Tucker sniffed to me about the time he was chased by coyotes. I can't think of anything scarier than that.

But then Tucker was rescued by humans, and he soon found his human, my Paw Andy. Well, now he was OUR Paw Andy!

It didn't take Tucker very long to get used to his new home. After just a few weeks, he was a happy dog, just like me. Together we ran around the backyard and chased lizards and shared treats. We played every day, and every night we slept next to each other, pooped out from a long, happy day.

Sometimes we did things we shouldn't. We jumped in mud puddles because it looked fun. We ate bugs to see how they tasted. (Not good.) We puppy-wrestled and chased rodents through the desert.

Now Andy had two dogs to love him and show him how to love, and together the three of us took long walks in the park or went swimming in the pool. But Mr. Hunter will tell you a secret. Paw Andy thinks that he got Tucker so that I could have a brother, but as you already know, the dog picks the human. Tucker had already picked Andy; it just took him longer to get here.

Remember in the last chapter, when Mr. Hunter said that we should be happy for all that we have? Well, now I had a brother, and I was very happy to have him. And now Tucker feels loved. We both give and receive love, and that is all we need. If you have brothers and sisters—even if they annoy you or frustrate you or make you angry—always be happy they're in your life!

chapter 9
Tucker's Tale

Love is a "two-way street." That means that loves goes out, and love comes in. It's not enough just to love others; you have to let yourself be loved, too! Take it from Mr. Hunter. You are loved, but for you to know that, you have to let those who love you show you how they love you!

One morning we woke up and found that T-Bear (that was my nickname for Tucker) was not hungry. I sniffed to Paw Andy that he seemed very tired and would not move much. Andy was very worried about him. Later that afternoon, Tucker still could not get up, so we took him to the veterinarian (a doctor for animals) to see what was wrong with him.

The vet doctors ran all kinds of tests on T-Bear. There was nothing that Paw Andy and I could do except wait and see what would happen. After a while, the vet came to us and said, "Tucker is very sick."

They told us that Tucker had to go to a special animal hospital, one of the very best in the whole world. Andy put T-Bear in the car and we drove as fast as we could. By this time, Tucker could barely move. He was not getting any better. All Mr. Hunter could do was lay by his side and let him know that he was loved.

Now I have to warn you that this part is very sad. We got to the special animal hospital and the vets there looked over T-Bear. They came to me and Paw Andy and they said, "We don't know if Tucker will last the night. You might want to say goodbye now, just in case."

They told us that Tucker had four different problems all at one time. My poor Paw's heart was breaking right in front of me! We both cried for Tucker and hoped that he would get better. Dogs know that it's okay to cry, no matter what humans say.

We waited and waited to see if T-Bear would get better. Then my Paw Andy got a phone call from a special friend named Mary who was an emergency nurse for people.

Mary said, "You must spend all the time you can with Tucker, and let him know you love him." Somehow Mary knew that if we shared our love with T-Bear, he would get better.

Every day Paw Andy would go visit Tucker at the animal hospital. He would sit with him and tell him, "Paw loves you, and needs you to get better."

Days and days went by, and it still didn't look like Tucker would get better. We hoped and prayed and loved him as much as we could.

Do you know what a miracle is? A miracle is when something amazing happens that you can't explain. And one morning a miracle happened for us too, when Tucker's vet Dr. Brown called my Paw Andy.

"Oh no, what is she going to say?" we thought.

Dr. Brown said, "I wanted to tell you that Tucker is getting better. It's a miracle!"

My Paw Andy shouted and cheered and danced! Tucker had a chance. I knew it was because we believed in him and loved him. It does not always work out this way, and that is why a miracle is so special.

It was eight more days before T-Bear could come home, but when he did, we were all so happy to be a complete family again. As Mr. Hunter says, a home is just not a home without a dog or two!

You see, it was our love for Tucker that showed him that he should get better. But I will tell you a secret. While Paw Andy was loving Tucker and helping to save his life, Tucker was also helping to save Andy's life. Tucker was showing him how to let go of all the other problems in his life, everything else in the world, and make a decision based on love.

Sharing love is one of the most important things you can do. Everything else should come second.

chapter 10
Every Day is a Gift

Mr. Hunter is an older dog now. I don't run around and play as much as I used to. I still love to take walks in the park, and I love to swim in the pool. I let Tucker chase all the lizards and rabbits and tennis balls. Each day I wake up happy, and each night I go to bed happy, because every day is a gift, and I know I am loved.

Mr. Hunter wants to give you one more lesson, and this last lesson might be the most important one of all. So far we have talked about how to love others, and how to be loved, but there is one other thing that you must always do, and that is you must love yourself.

Loving yourself is the greatest love of all. If you don't love yourself, you might have a hard time letting others love you, or believing that others can love you. No matter how people treat you or what they say, you must always love yourself more and be happy with yourself. You are a good person and all dogs love you!

When Mr. Hunter sniffs, "Love yourself," I don't mean to love the way you look, or love that you are the best at something. I mean that you have to love who you are as a person. You have to know that you are giving love and getting love. You have to know that you are happy with what you have, and you have to know that every day is a gift. Every person (and dog!) in your life is special. By loving them, you're being a part of something bigger.

So really, loving yourself is kind of a combination of all our other lessons rolled into one. If you love yourself, then you should know that you are doing everything else you can to love and be loved. If you forget how to love, you can always go hug a dog—we will remind you!

Please don't forget the tricks that Mr. Hunter has taught you in this book. And as we come to the end, here is one more trick. The next time you feel like you're alone, sad, angry, frustrated, or unloved, you can always pick up this book and read a tail or two to remind yourself that you are loved, always, and that by giving love, you will be loved.

I hope that you have enjoyed my tails, and I hoped that you have learned a thing or two about love. It really is the most important thing in the world. And of course, always remember to give your dog a big hug and a yummy peanut-butter treat. Woof!

With Love,
Mr. Hunter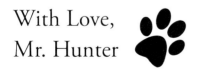

Questions for Parents and Children

The following section was created by Mr. Tucker, Hunter's Labrador brother in the Dedication page picture with Kathleen. Tucker wants to give parents and children an opportunity to discuss some of the important themes of each chapter. Test your imagination and have fun listening to the priceless expressing of your children . . . it's a super special gift just for you amazing parents!

Chapter 1: Hello, I'm Hunter!
Question: How would you explain what it is to feel loved, and then to share love with someone?

Chapter 2: Dogs and People . . . Who Really Chooses Who?
Question: What are some ways that I can show my doggie soul mate how much I love them?

Chapter 3: Puppy Love
Question: When I feel sad, frustrated or even angry, how can my puppy's love for me cheer me up?

Chapter 4: Healing for People and Dogs
Question: What would be some examples of giving love and receiving love that you are proud of?

Chapter 5: Would You Trade Your Troubles with Someone Else?
Questions: What kinds of things can I do to volunteer and help people who need my love and support?

Chapter 6: Be Part of Something Bigger
Question: What are some bigger choices in life that can really make other people feel loved by me?

Chapter 7: A Dog Only Needs His or Her Human
Question: How can I focus more on being thankful for what I have, instead of what I want?

Chapter 8: Hunter Gets a Brother!
Question: Why is it so important for my happiness to love my brothers and sisters and all family and friends?

Chapter 9: Tucker's Tale
Question: What are some examples of how you will choose to share love with someone else in need?

Chapter 10: Every Day is a Gift
Question: What can I do to love myself so that I have the courage to love others, and feel loved in return?

Whether you want to purchase bulk copies of Hunter's Tail
or buy another book for a friend, get it now at:
www.hunterstail.com

Find Hunter on Facebook:
www.facebook.com/HuntersTail

Follow Hunter on Twitter:
www.twitter.com/HuntersTail

CPSIA information can be obtained
at www.ICGtesting.com
Printed in the USA
LVXC01n0051241117
557346LV00008B/55